D0886697

OTWE

*Also by Verna Aardema*

TALES FROM THE STORY HAT

THE NA OF WA

THE SKY-GOD STORIES

# OTWE

by Verna Aardema

Illustrated by Elton Fax

Coward-McCann, Inc.     New York

*Otwe* is based upon "The Man and the Snake" by Ray Huffman in *Nuer Customs and Folklore,* 1931, published by the Oxford University Press. Reprinted by permission of the International African Institute.

*To little Maggie Roberts
who read this story first.*

N ear the Mountains of the Moon,
in Africa, there once lived a man named
Otwe.

Otwe was a happy man. A big laugh lived inside of him. He was a good man, too.

Happy and good!

But *that's* what got him into trouble! It happened like this:

One day Otwe saw a big snake fighting a little one. He took a stick and drove off the big snake.

The little snake said, "Thank you. You are kind. I'm going to give you a gift."

The snake gave Otwe a tiny feather.

"With this magic feather you will hear animals think," it said. "But you must not tell anyone."

Otwe took the feather and went home.

That night Loti, his wife, put the baby to sleep. Otwe locked the door, and they went to bed.

Soon they heard a mosquito going zing, zing, zing around the door.

Then Otwe heard the mosquito say to itself, "What is this world coming to! People lock their houses so well a poor, hungry traveler can't find a crack!"

Otwe laughed. He laughed so hard he fell out of bed.

"What's so funny?" asked Loti.

"Nothing," said Otwe. He could not tell
her.

Soon a rat tried the door. It could not get in either. But it found a hole under the roof and came in there.

Pat, pat went the little feet of the rat. Pat, pat, pat – up and down the house.

Then Otwe heard it say to itself, "Now, I wonder where that woman keeps her butter!"

Otwe laughed. He laughed so hard he scared the rat. And it jumped up onto Loti's bed.

"Wah!" cried Loti. "Get that rat off me!"

The rat jumped to the wall and scurried out through the hole under the roof.

"Otwe," said Loti. "I think your big laugh made that rat jump on me! What were you laughing about?"

"Nothing," said Otwe.

The next morning Otwe let the cow out of the shed and tied her to a post so Loti could milk her. Soon he saw his wife coming with her bowl.

The cow saw her, too. And Otwe heard her say to herself, "There comes that woman with her big bowl. She takes all my milk and my calf gets none. This time I just won't give any milk."

Otwe laughed. He laughed so hard he scared the cow. And she galloped around the post.

"What's wrong with you?" cried Loti. "Scaring the cow with your foolish laughter! Are you laughing at me?"

"No," said Otwe. "It was nothing."

The cow did not give milk. Loti didn't get a drop in her bowl.

The next day the cow still would not give milk.

Then Loti called Otwe. "Look," she said, "no milk! Our baby is crying for it. That calf is killing our daughter!"

The cow swung her big head around and looked at Loti. And Otwe heard her say to herself, "What? My daughter is killing her daughter?"

Otwe laughed. He laughed so loud that the cow kicked and sent the bowl rolling in the dirt.

"Now see what you did!" cried Loti.
"You and that foolish laugh! I'm going to
tell the chief."

Loti told the chief.

The chief called Otwe and all his wise men to the shade tree in the middle of the village.

All the people of the village came, too.

"Otwe," said the chief, "your wife tells me you laugh when there is nothing to laugh about. Is that true?"

"No," said Otwe. "I never laugh without a reason. But I can't tell the reason."

"He laughs at me," said Loti. "I'm the only one around."

"No," said Otwe. "It isn't that."

"If you do not laugh at your wife, what do you laugh about?" asked the chief.

Someone shouted, "Tell us, Otwe. We want to laugh, too."

"If you will not tell," said the chief, "your wife will have to take her things and go home to her father."

Otwe didn't want to lose his wife!

So, he told about the snake, the magic feather, and the funny thoughts of the animals.

Then he fell over dead.

"Look!" cried the oldest wise man. "We made him do what he should not have done. And he has had to pay with his life."

Loti and many of the people began to cry.

The chief shook his head sadly.

Suddenly the little snake came out of the grass. It put its shiny head on Otwe's head.

Otwe moved.

Then he began to laugh! For as he was coming back to life, he heard the snake say to itself, "Snoopy, that's what they are. Can't let a man keep a secret."

"Look!" cried the oldest wise man. "Otwe is alive again! And laughing!"

Then all the people began to laugh.

And Loti said, "Laugh all you want, Otwe. I'll never fuss about it again."